Harrowed Earth - Book One

Appalachian Blues

Aaron Conaway

A K&Q Press Publication

Front Cover Art Credit: Daniel Moler

"Harrowed Earth" logo created by Jeremy Bohannon

First Edition 2021

Books by Aaron Conaway

The Timberhaven Chronicles

Before the Weaver

Waking the Weaver

Monsters in the Park (Coming Soon!)

The Michael Gideon Collection

I Live Here Now

Spookhunt

Edimmu

Tales for Halloween

Table of Contents

The Way of the World: Part One

Earth.

The end of the 20th Century saw the rise of superheroes, which in turn were the harbingers of a golden age of humanity.

At the dawn of the 21st Century, alien races made themselves known on Earth, having secretly had a hand in humanity's technological advances for more than a hundred years. New Orleans rose far above the sea, a modern-day Atlantis in reverse. Scientific achievement exploded, bringing about cures for diseases of the body, mind, and spirit. Earth's people worked as one, hand-in-hand with the aliens toward these endeavors until the entirety of the solar system was within the grasp of a Unified Earth.

Then the true intentions of the alien races were made known. A galactic oligarchy working behind the scenes for countless years, the Ravok-Dyn, arrived in ships the size of nations to claim Earth as their own. Earth's super-powered warred against the Ravok-Dyn, culminating in the Pacific Ocean disappearing into a star-filled abyss of folded space. An event that the surviving inhabitants of Earth have since referred to as The Shift.

And the world fell.

But the people did not.

It's 2026, The Rocky Mountains in Colorado are now the western coastline of the U.S. due to The Shift, and of the small percent still on Earth when robbed of any claim of ownership, humanity is trying to find its way in this new world order. The aliens live above, the people below. Set back more than a century with the technology now available, on a planet where the light of the sun hardly reaches them, there are ever-changing counts of monsters in the dark.

Yet watch as they find their way.

Nomads: A small group of brave souls who traverse the remnants of the U.S., mapping the Unknown Land while seeking out scattered pockets of humanity in hopes of connecting settlements via radio transmissions.

Diggers: An exclusive guild, notoriously difficult to gain access to, Diggers are individuals who, through technical expertise, convert natural cave systems into underground cities.

What Bleeds, Dies

Unknown Land

West of Danville, Virginia PW (Pre-Worldfall)

Something was feeding noisily in the dark—something large, by the sounds of rending, gnashing, and slurping.

Jedidiah's motorcycle was some two miles back the way he'd come. This far into the Unknown Land, noise from the Fat Boy would have been deadly. Unfortunately, that made for poor exit strategy options.

The Unknown Land referred to the expanse of territory under the alien city-ships toppling above it, virtually the entire east coast of what had once been the United States. The air was poisonous to humans there, forcing Jedidiah to wear an air purifier—a small clear mask that covered his mouth, with two hoses that ran up into his nostrils, cupping over his nose at its top. The Unknown Land stayed dark as pitch and filled with terrors, both foreign and domestic, and would remain the Unknown Land unless Nomads like Jedidiah did their part to reclaim it for humans.

Jedidiah ran his hexed flashlight first left, then right, its beam scouring the surrounding dead brush and trees. The magics cast on it kept anyone, or anything, from seeing the light (if there was a spell that could do the same for motorcycles, he had yet to come across it), but the range of its beam was relatively limited. Whatever was out there lunching might still track his movement.

Jedidiah dispelled the flashlight and clicked his goggles, bringing night vision up with a whir. It was a massive drain on their limited battery power, but none of that would matter if Jedidiah got killed for moving about too much. He pivoted his head, slowly checking his surroundings. There was a small building buried in a foliage of some kind ten yards to his right. Great cover if it was unoccupied. And if whatever was eating was too busy to notice him go for it.

A wind picked up then, howling a lamentation born someplace in the south. Jedidiah grabbed the chance, hoping the wind would help cover his movement's sound, and walked toward the building. One step turned into three. Then a half-dozen more. Nothing seemed to be following, but Jedidiah no longer heard the sound of chewing either. He was near to the building; a dozen more steps would do it. But then he was on gravel, a road of some kind. The sound of his footsteps crunching over rocks blasted in his ears. How could whatever was out there not hear him as well?

His mind made up that the *something out there* had to have heard, Jedidiah ran for the building. He didn't stop until he touched the cinder block wall, a garage of some kind? Racing around the edge, feeling his way, Jedidiah came upon a closed door, wider than it was tall. He began to look through one of its six small windows to see what was inside when his goggles *beooo*ed out loudly into the dark. Dead. Jedidiah couldn't see anything but black for all the good his unaided eyes were doing him.

Jedidiah knelt before the garage door, trying to become as small as possible. He slowly moved his hands under his flannel shirt to one of the leather pouches at his belt. He pushed his face against the wood of the door, trying to listen for any sounds coming from behind it. The wind slowed its moaning then, and Jedidiah heard the heavy footsteps from back the way he'd come. They were getting closer with each breath he took until, finally, his nimble fingers untied the leather pouch he was after.

The problem with magic, or at least the brand of magic that Jedidiah practiced, was that it was only properly effective—whether in aid or against—those attached to the same natural laws. Denizens of Hell, earthbound spirits, these things Jedidiah could combat when necessary with his various tools of the trade because the walls keeping demons and ghosts separate from humanity each shared a window with Earth.

But the further one went into the Unknown Land, the more likely things living there followed *different* sets of laws. Alien creatures attuned to alien planets, with their own subculture of infernal, which could sometimes make Jedidiah's magical options a bit dodgy in situations such as the one he currently found himself in.

Jedidiah could hear his pursuer crossing the gravel road edging closer still. Whether it was tracking him by scent or some profane ability, Jedidiah couldn't say, but he couldn't wait any longer. He pulled a honeysuckle flower from his pouch and pinched it between his thumb and finger, whispering to the wooden garage door as he did. The spell wouldn't have worked on the cinder blocks—there was nothing left of their original components that remembered what it had once been. Besides, rocks were too stubborn to be swayed—but, though repurposed, the wooden door Jedidiah might be able to sweet talk. Trees had long memories and enjoyed the attention.

The sounds of impending danger closing in grew to include heavy labored breathing. Jedidiah had heard tales of creatures from the stars that had made their home in the Atlantic, sometimes coming inland to give birth. Gigantic beasts, resembling earth-born crocodiles the size of whales if Jedidiah were to believe their description.

He found it easier to believe at the moment, though, accompanied by the monstrous breathing coming around the corner toward him.

Then the wood of the door gave way, folding him inside and through into the garage as it sealed itself back up again behind him. He paused, laying on a cold stone floor for the length of three deep breaths of his own, and then rose to his feet. Though he knew full well that his eyes were unable to adjust in the absence of any light at all, Jedidiah peeked out through where he felt the window to be. Inhaling deeply in disbelief, he knew something outside moved by the garage door. Something slow, heavy, and large. A black mass that was darker than the dark, sliding across his vantage point.

* * * * *

Jedidiah counted to three hundred before even thinking about leaving the garage's relative safety, and even then, he opted to explore his surroundings first. He felt around the ground in the immediate vicinity, trying to see his sanctuary by touch. Many small pieces of metal, unfamiliar to his fingers and sharp along their edges, lie scattered. There was a large cloth of some kind, coarse and riddled with holes, as well.

Though he waited nearly another ten minutes more beforehand, Jedidiah finally turned his hexed light back on, careful to do so once he was away from where he knew the windowed door to be. The room he found himself in revealed itself among pitched shadows and swirling dust, the former running from his flashlight while the latter danced within its purview. A half-dismantled vehicle of some kind was to his right, with two of its four wheels missing and no discernible roof. Chains hung from the ceiling through a network of pulleys and cranks.

Standing, Jedidiah shone the light down, trying to avoid kicking any of the metal shards he'd felt. On closer look, they appeared to be bolts shorn clean from something heavy and oversized. The sudden sound of loud breathing made him look up in time to see the machinery flying down at him. Jedidiah dove to his right, rolling behind a nearby shelf for cover as shrapnel exploded all around the room with a booming crash.

Decades of dust blew out from the wreckage and coated the room in a fog that Jedidiah's flashlight couldn't penetrate, so, clicking it off, he sat and listened as the room quieted around him, ready to jump away again at the slightest noise. The sound of movement near the ceiling drew his attention upward, though he could see nothing in the dark. He turned his light back on.

A piercing screech ripped out, followed by a flurry of something large scurrying across the catwalk railing that hung from the ceiling. It made its way around a corner and out of Jedidiah's sight.

Not as big as whatever was outside, Jedidiah thought, searching for another exit. *But still, not something I want at my back.*

He shuffle-crawled out from around the shelf and crept around a bench, keeping the beam of his flashlight moving in search of every corner he came across as he went. More crashing came from around the bend to his left, so Jedidiah hugged the wall to his right, opening another pouch at his belt while keeping his flashlight trained toward the noise as he approached the corner.

The garage opened up into a T-shape at the end of the hall, and Jedidiah eased to its edge, hoping that his light wouldn't find danger before he was finished preparing his spell. He pulled blue ash from the pouch and coated his palm with the residue, whispering incantations to ready his attack. The light caught another opening then, just at the end of the new hall, a gaping hole where a wall should be.

Jedidiah's stomach sank at the realization. His sanctuary was not safe at all.

As if cued by Jedidiah's understanding, something moved across the light's beam. It was a leg. A giant leg attached to a creature that Jedidiah did not want to get to know further.

I can double-back and make it out the garage door before it gets back around front, Jedidiah thought. He turned around, toward the way he'd come, and was met with another piercing screech.

A monstrosity the like of which Jedidiah had never seen was caught in his flashlight's beam. Reared back in that instant as it was, the creature appeared to Jedidiah to be a mismatch of random animals. It had a primate's body, like a gorilla of the old world, only completely hairless. In place of an ape's head, though, a second torso extended outward from the neck, with two praying mantis arms and a diamond-shaped head filled with buggy eyes and an extended mouth full of teeth. It swiped one of its insect arms at Jedidiah's chest, slashing him as it skittered away out of the light and back up to the ceiling.

Could've killed me, Jedidiah cursed his own stupidity at gawking at the thing. He touched his hand to his chest, and blood came away with it.

Seeing the blue ash there as well made him remember that he wasn't unarmed.

"**Cavoto!**" He yelled, pointing his hand to the ceiling. Three blue plumes of fire shot from Jedidiah's hand, blowing the top of the roof off the garage and setting fire to most of the hall underneath. He ran for the garage door, doing his best to not trip over anything as he went. Sparing a look back, he saw that the diamond head was charging behind him—and away from the gigantic toothy maw tearing through the crumbling hall behind *it*.

The size of this second new creature filled the hall, flames lighting its massive head as everything burned around it. The monstrosity slung its head left and right, destroying everything in its path in pursuit of fresh meat, the garage crumbling in its wake.

"We'd hardly be a mouthful!" Jedidiah yelled over his shoulder as the diamond head skittered up the wall to his left and onto the ceiling, racing toward the garage door as well. The smaller beast outpaced Jedidiah easily, blasting through the wood and glass in its hurry.

"Sonuva—" was all Jedidiah got out before the world exploded behind him, flinging his body into the dark after the diamond head in a concussive blast full of smoke and fire. He threw his arms up, trying to protect his head and face, coming perilously close to a tree as he rag-dolled his way end over end to the ground.

Marking the pain as intense but bearable, Jedidiah rolled to his side and looked back toward what was left of the garage. The giant monster, for Jedidiah honestly couldn't think of anything else to call it at that moment, was bellowing in rage and pain, standing a full head taller than the burning wreckage of the garage. It *was* built somewhat crocodile-shaped, Jedidiah noted the rumors, only this creature was leviathan size, with thick, wet, sinewy tendrils slithering around its mouth. Its teeth were half as tall as Jedidiah, and it had at least three pairs of stubby legs that Jedidiah could see, holding up its terrible frame. It didn't seem to find the burning building it was standing in bothersome, but whatever had exploded inside had done some damage because bloody wounds were gushing from its side.

Jedidiah moved his hand, now more gingerly since narrowly surviving an explosion, to his pouch, unsure of what, exactly, he was going to do against such reckless destruction, when a heavy blade stabbed down, pinning his flannel shirt into the ground.

Jedidiah looked up into the face of the diamond head as it pulled its praying mantis arm back to its side. It made a soft, weird noise, like it had rattlesnakes in its mouth, then looked back up at the terror from its hiding spot.

The beast roared again, flinging its head about in frustration. It stepped out of the wreckage, lumbering forth with at least two of its left legs mangled and dragging, and sniffed first the air, then the ground.

Well, that's not good, Jedidiah thought. He looked back to the diamond head only to find an empty spot at the tree line where it had been.

Jedidiah moved slowly, ever so slowly, not taking

his eyes off of the beast as he slid back toward those

same trees. It felt safe enough to get to a crouching

position once he broke through the brush, so

Jedidiah got to his feet. The beast was coming

toward his hiding place, though. Slowly, at first.

Seeking the trail of his scent? Jedidiah wasn't sure,

but it seemed that way. Then the creature stopped,

lifted its head up, and charged toward Jedidiah.

In one fluid motion, Jedidiah reached a hand

to his belt, pulled out a small handful of something

that, under lamplight, would look like pepper, and

flung it toward the beast's head. Jedidiah quickly

turned his face and shouted, "**Balmbados!**'

Dozens of little lights exploded around the

beast's head, blinding it momentarily. The beast

roared, enraged, as Jedidiah ran into the forest of

dead trees to the sound of the tentacles around its mouth lashing about behind him. The further Jedidiah ran from the burning garage, the less he could easily navigate the dark, dense forest. He cursed himself, silently, upon finding that his hexed flashlight seemed to have been lost in the garage escape. He impatiently tried his goggles again, knowing the result would be the same.

Too bad batteries don't recharge when getting blown out of buildings.

Branches whipping about his face forced Jedidiah to slow down, but trees falling down behind him quickened his pace once again. Hoping that he wasn't wholly disoriented in retreat, Jedidiah began working his way left as he ran, in hopes of getting on a course that led him back to the Fat Boy.

But then the noises of his pursuer died down behind him. Something had happened, back in the forest. Jedidiah, fighting the urge to just keep running, turned toward the commotion. The beast had been diverted, it seemed, and was contending with new prey.

"Oh, man," Jedidiah said.

He had inadvertently run the creature right into the diamond head's hiding spot. The diamond head was caught up in the beast's tentacles, being dragged toward a grim death in its cavernous mouth. The diamond head fought off its intended fate. The massive arms of its middle half fended off the tentacles—it had even pulled one utterly free of the beast's face—while its upper praying mantis arms cut and slashed in quick movements, covering the scene in the beast's viscous blood. But Jedidiah knew he was about to watch the diamond head's end as the dry, sun-starved forest burned down around them.

I could run, he thought. *This would give me all the time I needed to get out of here.*

Knowing that's not how things would play out, Jedidiah *did* run, only back *toward* the battle to the death that was taking place, digging into his front pocket as he went. It was all of the beast's blood that gave him the idea. It was true that his magic performed unpredictably when it came to aliens—and he had no doubt that both the beast and the diamond head were aliens—cause and effect should come into play regardless.

As he drew closer, some fifty feet away from the ordeal, Jedidiah watched as one of the beast's large eyes spun to take in his approach, even as it continued trying to eat the diamond head. It roared, tentacles gouging into the sides of the diamond head while its prey shrieked, slashing and rending its attacker. Trees fell, both due to fire and by the battle at hand, as smoke began to fill their makeshift arena.

"Hold tight, Diamond Head!" Jedidiah yelled, even though he assumed the act was futile. "Here goes nothing," he said, under his breath as he drew a black harmonica from his pocket and to his lips.

That the instrument had magical tendencies could not be in doubt. And Jedidiah was a mage of some standing, in multiple circles, in this overthrown and conquered planet that he called home. But, the song he played then was born of two parts hope and one part spontaneous curiosity.

As the harmonica's song tore out through the night, the atmosphere changed through the fire, fight, and smoke. It began to feel energized, as though a thunderstorm of old was coming. The air smelled rank, like something died nearby, its corpse uneaten and left too long to the elements. Jedidiah didn't know where they'd appear. He'd only heard that particular song once, its magic neither performed by him, nor had he been the intended target. That time. But he knew they would come and that they would hunt what bled until it no longer bled.

Hellhounds.

The first came up from behind the beast, hardly reaching to the knee of the creature's smallest back legs. The following two seemingly lept from the flames in front of the battling aliens.

The three after that were already attacking the creature atop its back by the time Jedidiah noticed them. Jedidiah kept playing, though, until he had a baker's dozen sicced on the beast. Thirteen little monsters to distract one giant one.

That worked?! Jedidiah thought as he finished playing. The creature dropped the diamond head in its fury at the small—from its perspective—dogs nipping at its legs, neck, head, and belly. A hellhound ripped off one of the behemoth's wounded legs, running off with it before coming in for more. The diamond head began to slowly climb-crawl away from the scene, large gouges in its sides, just beneath its middle arms.

"Diamond Head, this way!" Jedidiah said, shouting over the roars of the creature, driven mad with irritation but not looking to Jedidiah's eyes much worse for wear. The diamond head hissed as the mage approached closer but let itself be helped to its feet.

"I know, I know," Jedidiah said. "Let me make it up to you by getting us out of here."

The diamond head, limping, put one of its fleshy, muscular arms over Jedidiah's shoulder, trying to steady its walk to a trot to put more distance between them and the creature. Jedidiah felt his skin crawl at the diamond head's touch. Its flesh felt clammy and rough, as though fine hairs pricked at Jedidiah's neck.

Ugh, he thought. *That's . . . unpleasant.* He sighed, resigning himself to the situation. *Now, let's hit the road.*

* * * * *

It took a while to get back to relative safety. The diamond head had forced them to stop near the garage on the way at what Jedidiah presumed was the site of where fellow members of its party had become the behemoth's recent meal. There weren't many body parts left, but what there were resembled the same pale, wormlike flesh. The diamond head chittered its rattlesnake chitter quietly for a moment and then wanted to go.

Jedidiah led them on.

Once they were to the Fat Boy, Jedidiah pulled some linen gauze strips out of a pouch on the back of the bike.

"Let me dress those," he said, pointing to the diamond head's wounds. The diamond head just sat down in the dirt and lifted its middle arms, resolved to its fate.

"I'm sorry about your people," Jedidiah said. He assumed that the alien had no idea what he was saying, but he hoped his tone could be read. "Anyhow." He finished dressing the wounds and got back into his bag. "We should be okay here. It's close enough to the edge of the Unknown Land that we could even have a small campfire. Rest for a while."

The diamond head chittered quietly again, lowering its arms and folding its praying mantis appendages to its side. It tilted its head slightly to the right, then the left, chittering once more and then laying down.

"Yeah," Jedidiah said. "Me too."

When the Dead Sing: Dream

Echoes in a vast canyon painted purple-blue beneath a lonesome moon suggest that it's not just the wind that's howling. "Ancient blood predates the old stories being repeated in Border Town. What treks unseen through hunting paths?"

"I'm dreaming," Jedidiah reasoned. Chiding himself for the thought, he cautiously emptied his mind to not broadcast any further thoughts. The Dreaming was a tricky place that way.

The unknown voice continued. "Anguish muted by quick teeth and stuporous venom means supper's on the table. Beware, you don't land in a similar state."

Jedidiah shot awake, sitting upright next to his still-warm campfire. Two nights in a row, his dream had been the same: a large, tree-filled canyon hosting a beast on the hunt and hungry. A stranger's voice, whispering warning. Up in Border Town.

Jedidiah looked around for the diamond head but wasn't overly surprised to find the creature gone already. The bits of linen Jedidiah had used to bandage the creature's wounds were roughly arranged in a bundle near the fire.

I must be beat, he thought. *I slept right through his goodbyes.*

Jedidiah stretched his arms out, rolled his neck around to stave off cricks, and then got to his feet. He was supposed to recon the Unknown Land for another three days, per this latest Nomad tour.

Change of plans.

Spirit Road

Hidden Hills, Back Canyon region

West of Roanoke, Virginia PW (Pre-Worldfall)

::TOXICITY LEVEL APPROACHING **SAFE** IN 3

KM::

The mystic clicked his recharged goggles,

sending the message away, and opened the throttle a

little more. The Fat Boy responded accordingly,

racing down what was once known as U.S. Route

81. Jedidiah Coalstream smiled, his poncho

billowing behind him so hard that his hood flew

back. There weren't many places he could race so

fast any longer. Most of the Old Roads were grown

over, wild. But this stretch always brought a grin to

Jedidiah's face.

As was typically the case this far into The Hidden Hills, the sky was dark, even though it was roughly 3:30 in the afternoon by Jedidiah's estimate. Natural light had a hard time of it in this part of the world anymore, at least so far as Jedidiah had traveled, and that was far indeed. Ever since the aliens showed up, took out Earth's defenses, and conquered everything with their city-ships, that was the end of regularly seeing the sun, the stars, the whole damn sky even though he was barely into the Back Canyon.

He was heading back toward lived-in country after a journey east of exploring some more of the world, trying to help the Unknown Land take up a little less space on his map. There hadn't been a human soul for two hundred miles or better back the way he came. It was too dangerous, back in the cold, black dark.

::TOXICITY LEVELS: **SAFE** - AIR QUALITY: **BREATHABLE**::

Jedidiah slowed his bike, feeling a pang of regret at doing so, and pulled to a stop in the road. Kickstand lowered, Jedidiah removed his breathing filter and took a deep breath. The air still smelled of ozone and tasted like copper, but that was what passed for normal in a world that lived under alien spacecraft. At least now that breath wouldn't kill him.

Jedidiah put his breathing gear in his bike's tote, then removed and did likewise with his helmet. He looked down and noticed the fuel needle was a little closer to **E** then he preferred, so he also removed his poncho, pulled out the plastic combination pad that was tucked behind the base of its hood, and entered the code: 1 4 2 2 3 3.

As the poncho began to beep, Jedidiah reached back into his bike's tote and pulled out a small, metallic piece of equipment, attaching it to the fuel cap on the motorcycle. A second typed-in code powered up the device, and then Jedidiah connected his poncho through a series of tubes, finishing the procedure.

The air to the east wasn't breathable due to the alien world above raining contaminants into the atmosphere. Still, one quick conversion later, those same particles in the air granted Jedidiah fuel for the Fat Boy.

Shivering slightly, Jedidiah got into the satchel strapped onto the back of his motorcycle and pulled out a heavy flannel. The Hidden Hills' temperature topped out at around fifty-two degrees during waking hours, thrust into perpetual dark autumn all year long as it was. A friend of Jedidiah's, Yewell, claimed that she had bathed in cavern lakes that were warmer than Hidden Hills, though Jedidiah's fear of enclosed spaces meant he'd never be able to confirm the claim. Yewell was a Digger, tradespeople just outside of The Kingdom—a collection of baronies some nine hundred kilometers to the west—who spent their lives excavating and maintaining cavern networks inside mountains and beneath the earth. The thought of living that way made Jedidiah shiver again.

But then, a flash of movement to his immediate right made him think that it might be something else giving him goosebumps. It was an arm, floating independently about five feet from the road, etched in a light blue light. Translucent, for the most part, save for the hand at its end, which seemed solid. Above and slightly to the left of the arm, two eyes peeked from a glowing yellow cloud. Then another pair, further to Jedidiah's left, almost flanking him, followed by the appearance of a solitary mouth, screaming silently just above him.

Another body part appeared, then another—each born of an eerie yellow or blue light and seeming to keep proximity to the road.

"What's this then," Jedidiah whispered, tying his satchel closed. He crouched at the side of the road next to his motorcycle. He absently picked at some brush at the road's edge as his eyes darted, catching each spectral appearance, each movement.

Another specter, this one nearly an entire upper torso—minus its left arm and head—emerged into existence as though painted there by the wind in that same peculiar blue light. It appeared next to Jedidiah wearing a strange jacket. Stenciled across the back were the letters **INM**. As soon as the half-ghost arrived, the disembodied arms, hands, eyes, and feet began to hover closer to the highway, almost in rhythm.

Jedidiah inhaled a breath as the brush near his feet faded to dust, even the piece in his hand. He understood then how this stretch of Old Road was always such a smooth ride. It was the Why of it that was escaping him. He took the harmonica out of the back pocket of his blue jeans. A flash of blue light from the ghost's reflection shone across the instrument's black metal as Jedidiah brought the harmonica up to his lips. He didn't play, though.

Not yet.

The grotesquerie of bloodless organs and appendages maneuvered around the road, tending it as Jedidiah watched. There were roughly a half-dozen malformed people, by the count of body parts, and the **INM** torso seemed to be in charge of the lot. When it moved on to the next road spot, the rest followed, clearing every bit of brush and debris and repairing any cracks that they came across.

Jedidiah had been about to play one tune but changed his mind. He blew another song instead. The air all around the scene began to spark and move with tiny streaks of silver-white electricity at the whim of the harmonica's music. At a turn, the various body parts began to take on entire bodies. Still transparent and oddly lit in death lights, but whole. Seven spirits that used to be people stood around Jedidiah once his song finished. Men of various builds, demeanor, and levels of awareness.

The man in the **INM** jacket—though it turned out

that it wasn't a jacket. He and all of the others wore

coveralls, and that *all* of them read **INMATE** on the

back—looked straight at Jedidiah. He had been tall.

Bald, with a goatee.

"There's no need for you all to stay here,"

Jedidiah offered, finally taking the harmonica away

from his mouth. He spoke as if the ghosts could

hear him. Experience told him they could. "I've got

a pretty good idea why you're doing what you're

doing, but that world is gone. Whatever debts you

owed, I'd say they've been paid."

The big, bald inmate dropped a nod at

Jedidiah. Then waved a hand at his fellow inmates,

who, following where he led, made their way onto

the next spot to clean on the Old Road.

Jedidiah watched them wander off, briefly wondering if they chose not to move on out of worry for what that entailed for them. Fear of the devil keeping them locked into an eternity of servitude in long, dark chains that didn't exist anymore. But, as he finished up his refuel, the Fat Boy now registering **F**, and put away his gear, Jedidiah decided that maybe it didn't have anything to do with what comes after. Could be what's owed is what's owed even if the world ends. Maybe especially then.

And that's all there is to it.

Respecting that, Jedidiah climbed back onto his motorcycle, fired it up, and headed down the road.

When the Dead Sing: Nightmare

Jedidiah knelt tending a small pan of sliced potatoes and onions in his campfire, the smell wafting up causing his stomach to rumble. He eyed his supper, testing it with a pocketknife and gauging it not quite finished, and sat back, crossing his long legs before him. He wiped the knife clean on his pants, folded it closed, and put it in his pocket. Watching first the pan's contents and then looking into the fire in which they cooked, Jedidiah reached into the breast pocket of his flannel shirt.

His black harmonica.

The instrument was a powerful talisman. Arguably Jedidiah's signature weapon, if such things still mattered in the world, but Jedidiah never saw it as such. It was home, was the black harmonica. It could bring joy every much as it could cause chaos.

Though he couldn't say for sure why he decided to prove the fleeting notion, Jedidiah brought the instrument to his lips and played. It was a newer melody, one he'd learned from a traveling blade peddler on the road maybe two years back.

"It'll ward off melancholy," the peddler had said as he taught the tune. "And bad dreams."

Jedidiah played as his supper cooked.

He began soft and slow at first, dancing the notes out like shy children at Maker's Feast before the guests. Not content, Jedidiah continued playing, picking up the pace a little. The once shy children were now skipping and jumping, dancing with briefly forgotten cousins now remembered. The fire crackled and popped, joining in on the song as

Jedidiah watched the flames sway in orange, red, and yellow. His eyes ran down, down the flames toward the three burnings logs inside his small ring of stones.

In their charcoaling embers, Jedidiah saw two eyes looking back at him.

He wasn't disturbed by the turn of events, oddly. He wasn't really even overly surprised, certainly not enough to stop playing his song. As though strange eyes staring out at a person cooking their dinner was the norm. One eye was deep purple, the other light teal. Both were unblinking.

The smoke from the campfire began to billow down instead of up, as was customary, and went on to form a small head in which to frame the eyes. Then one of the logs split, splintering into an approximation of a mouth, finishing the collage.

"Hail, **Moonlit Traveler**," the noseless fire-face spoke. "**Hail, Chaosbringer. Hail, Motorcycle Mystic.**"

Jedidiah kept playing his jaunty tune.

The fire jumped higher, nearly a foot. It swelled as well, beginning to consume the pan of food within. The eyes were now almost as high as Jedidiah's, though the burning log mouth was still at the base of the fire.

"**You do well not to speak**," the face in the fire said. "**Though your reputation suggested you weren't a fool.**"

Jedidiah's song continued unabated.

"**A word of suggestion**," said the fire. "**The Dreaming has polluted your mind, and you don't understand what you're coming toward; what *I* am. Only that you must see to it, and *me*. Your** sense of justice is . . . misguided in this case. We could just talk, you and I. I would very much enjoy that conversation. I've no need to see you dead, so much wasted potential. I could kill you now, were that the case."

The fire swelled again, completely melting the pan of food and all of its contents. Jedidiah's face and hands began to sting at the heat's proximity as sweat began to run down his face, yet still, he played.

"But I abhor using energy unnecessarily," the voice in the flames said, now eye to eye with Jedidiah. "And missed opportunities. Well, what's it to be? I can feel you coming closer from the south. Will you sit with me, or—"

The radio from Jedidiah's motorcycle beeped then, loudly in the dark. Someone was calling for help. The radio signal was strong, meaning that its source was within thirty miles at the furthest but probably closer.

The momentary disturbance reset the scene, except now the campfire was all but burnt out. Jedidiah realized that he was still playing his harmonica when his radio beeped again. Standing, he kicked the remnants of his dinner into the ring of stones, causing smoke to billow up from the wreckage.

Don't come to Border Town, a slight breeze whispered from within the smoke.

Jedidiah walked over to his motorcycle to find out what his next stop was.

He already knew where the stop after that would be.

Dark Offerings

Border Town region

Southeast of Charleston, West Virginia, PW

(Pre-Worldfall)

There are one and ten brave souls, waiting beneath the moon. Clara, their only teacher, went missing last Wednesday after church choir practice. They found her car abandoned at the edge of a nearby creek, keys in the ignition. Nothing missing except Clara.

The mountains, surrounding, whistling a dead man's tune in the crisp, cold air. One and ten souls, braver than most, standing guard in the shadows of their campfires, waiting beneath the moon. A cracking log, spitting embers into the night, signaling the stars, saying, "Wait, wait for me!" as a little brother left behind.

There is a motorcycle rumbling, coming up the country road, interrupting the mountains' whistling. Its rider arriving is emboldening one and ten brave souls to ask of themselves more than they ever have, waiting beneath the moon. One brave soul, head covered in a Coca-Cola hat, standing before the ten others, addressing them in the firelight.

"I told you he'd come. Jackie, get the hemp ready. We're going to save your sister."

A young woman is digging in her backpack as the rider is approaching. As she's pulling out a length of rope, the motorcycle is stopping before the one and ten brave souls gathered in anticipation beneath the moon. The rider is pulling off his helmet, turning off the bike, and then extending an arm to the approaching man in the Coca-Cola hat.

"Mr. Coalstream," the man in the Coca-Cola hat is saying, clasping the rider's forearm, "I can't thank you enough for coming. I didn't know who else to turn to. Who else to get involved with . . . well, with what we're dealing with here."

Getting off his motorcycle, the rider is replying, "No need for formalities. Jedidiah's fine. You've got the fires burning oil?" Jedidiah's asking, looking around the area. "Five pits, all burning oil and birch wood?"

"We do, sir," the girl called Jackie is answering, holding up her small length of rope while trying to put loose strands of hair behind her ear, "and I've got the hemp rope here. Three feet is all you needed?"

The man, Jedidiah, taking the rope from Jackie, examining it carefully, seeming satisfied, is walking around Jackie. Ignoring her, Jedidiah is looking around at the other faces of this group, checking their fingertips and sniffing their hair. He is taking the hemp rope and sweeping along the ground until dust clouds, like frenzied freed spirits, are dancing amidst the smoke of the fires.

A wolf is howling in the forest of the mountains. Followed by a second wolf. There's a third. Now a chorus of wolves, howling at the night, at the moon, at those standing around the fires. A flicker of fear is passing among the one and ten brave souls. If fear is in Jedidiah, it is not showing.

Jedidiah is positioning the men and women of this group two to a flame, having them sit cross-legged with the fire between them. He is placing Jackie in the middle of the circle of fires.

"Can't I be by a fire? I want to help." Jackie is saying tearing up as she does so.

Jedidiah is pulling some cloth from his pocket and wiping his hands with it. Looking into Jackie's eyes, he is folding the fabric into a long triangle and now tying it around the top of his head. The howling wolves sound closer. There is anger in their song.

"Clara is trapped, Jackie, but I know she can still hear what's happening now."

Jedidiah is circling, slowly circling, Jackie. The whites of his eyes begin slowly disappearing into the darkness of his skin, looking to Jackie like his dark pupils are expanding, making her feel afraid.

"Wh–what are you doing?" she is asking Jedidiah, spinning along with him as he is circling her.

The wolves sound closer still. Their high-pitched wails sounding more and more like dead things, hiding outside of the fire's light, explaining their torment in the only way they know how. Jedidiah is taking a step away from Jackie now, reaching into his back pocket.

"You were too jealous of Clara, weren't you, Jackie? You felt stuck in a small town with no prospects and no talent, didn't you?" Jedidiah is pulling a black harmonica from his pocket. "But Clara, she's a different story. She has the love of the community. Suitors lined up from here to two regions over." He is blowing a quick, sad note on the black harmonica.

Jackie is fondling the stretch of rope, looking nervously to see if the others can hear as they sit catatonic by their fire pits. The wailing of wolves is upon them. Jackie is suddenly looking over Jedidiah's shoulder to almost see a small, red-skinned man, his gray hair in long braids, standing naked just outside the edge of the firelight, melding with the night shadows, mixing between physical form and nightmare. Feeling empowered, Jackie is no longer needing to keep up pretenses.

"I hated Clara," Jackie is smiling a toothy smile, "so much. She had what I wanted, so I offered her up to any dark god that would have her. Now, she's gone, and people will notice me."

"I've nearly undone what you did to your sister." Jedidiah is grim, "Novices always mess up their offerings. You really shouldn't have played with magic."

"Novices?!" Jackie is laughing a crazed cackle to the heavens, "You think *I'm* a novice? I may not have understood what your little plan was tonight, but it isn't going to work! *This* is nylon, stupid! It isn't hemp rope!" Jackie is trying to throw the length of rope at Jedidiah. She is looking confused at the rope staying attached to her hand.

"I know." Now Jedidiah is playing the black harmonica. A blues tune never meant for the ears of man.

"What is happening? What are you doing?! Stop!" Jackie is screaming as the rope is working its way over her fingers, consuming its way down her arm like a half-starved constrictor. Her shoulder is popping, dislocating as the rope swallows its way toward her head and over, muffling her screams and finally bursting her skull. Within a minute, the being known as Jackie is gone, leaving in her place only a length of rope.

Jedidiah is ending his song on the black harmonica. He is walking over to where the rope is and picking it up, heading to the edge of the firelight with it. There, the almost man is holding out its almost hand. Jedidiah is giving it the length of rope that is now Jackie.

"I already have someone waiting for Clara at the creek where you got her. Clara better be there. Don't forget," Jedidiah is saying, tapping the black harmonica in his hand, "I know other songs."

The almost man is giving a slow nod and disappearing back into the mountains, the sound of rattlesnakes slithering on sand its accompaniment.

The brave souls, who now only number ten, are beginning to move in the fresh morning light as if they are waking from a deep sleep. The man in the Coca-Cola hat, seeing that Jackie is no longer among them, knows that the plan worked. That this stranger with the black harmonica saved Clara.

He must keep his gratitude, though, or whisper it into the wind.

The man known as Jedidiah Coalstream is gone.

When the Dead Sing: Story's End

Border Town region

West of Scio, Ohio, PW (Pre-Worldfall)

Darwyn Hess rocked back and forth, perched atop the Montgomerys' house behind a chimney. It had taken ages to scale the three-story home, but she finally managed it. Why this house? Darwyn never figured that out. Though truth be told, she hadn't put a lot of thought into it. All that mattered was that she was where she was meant to be.

She hugged her knees to her chest with her left arm while staring intently at her right hand, marveling at her brain's ability to control it. She flexed her fingers and pivoted her wrist as though casting an arcane spell from her dreams.

Darwyn stopped at the thought of her dreams, wrapped her right arm around her knees in solidarity with her left, and continued rocking.

Dreams invaded Darwyn's rest and had for months. Her face was sunken during the waking hours, with shadows springing up around her eyes and beneath her cheekbones. Her stare had become vacant, to the point where people had taken to avoiding her altogether.

Things were different in Darwyn's dreams, however.

In her dreams, Darwyn's world was in full color. Dressed in the vibrant shades of an Earth pre-Worldfall, trees, rivers with waterfalls, and the sun shining overhead. All things she'd only heard of in stories. And Darwyn was never a sickly teen while asleep, but an archmage who wielded mighty magic–spells and energies not seen by man for millennia. There, Darwyn had but to raise her arms to fly.

All is power within my hand, Darwyn thought, as she caught herself once again staring at her right hand. Then, as if signaled, Darwyn stood, walked to the edge of the roof, raised her arms, and jumped.

She did not fly.

* * * * *

Jedidiah rode toward the small village slowly, his eyes searching both flanks carefully. Dreams and visions warning him to stay away notwithstanding, it was a good habit whenever entering a new space. One never knew what was waiting in the world.

Any citizens within a village space, no matter the size, kept themselves behind tall, sturdy fences if they wanted any chance of surviving. Monsters in the dark didn't always wait until dark to steal your life. Nor did they always *appear* as monsters. Sometimes they showed up looking just like you. So Jedidiah wasn't surprised when he pulled up to a stop at a closed wooden gate, guarded by two sentries.

"You don't see a lot of wooden ones anymore," Jedidiah said, taking off his helmet and motioning to the gate with it. He didn't move to get off the Fat Boy, though. "The upkeep must be extensive."

"Oh, you wouldn't believe–" the guard on the left, a woman with a machete, began, a prideful smile on her lips.

"Ett!" her counterpart, another woman, this one wielded a spear, interrupted the first with a stern glance. The guard armed with a spear turned to Jedidiah. "What's your business today, sir?"

Sir? Jedidiah noted the unusual professionalism, particularly in a profession where gruffness is the more common flavor, but opted to move things along. "I'm a Nomad, here to offer my services." He pulled a small silver chain from around his neck out from under his shirt. It had a circle with three squiggly lines inside of it, the symbol of the Nomads. "Check on any news or updates you might have. Is the magistrate available?"

"Understood, sir," the spear guard said with a curt nod. "Unfortunately, no, the magistrate is tied up currently. There's been an accident, and she's tending to things with the family."

"I hope it's nothing serious," Jedidiah said, casually getting off his motorcycle and stowing his helmet. He then pulled his poncho back, folding it over his shoulder to show that he wasn't armed, though he hadn't been asked to do so, per the custom in that scenario. Jedidiah could see the spear guard note what he'd done and then quickly squint her eyes as though chiding herself for missing an easy question on a test.

"A young woman fell from a roof," the machete guard spoke up. "Her wounds have been tended to as best we can, but," she looked to the spear guard, clearly the higher ranking of the two, to see whether she should continue. No reprimand came. "It's been four days, and . . . she hasn't woken up yet." She said the last looking down.

"I'm sorry to hear it," Jedidiah said, offering his condolences with a bowed head. "Why don't I stop back by this way after I finish up on the east side of Border Town to check in with the magistrate then?"

"We would appreciate that sir," Spear guard said.

"Would it be okay if I came in long enough to rest my bike, though? Maybe trade for something to eat?" Jedidiah asked.

"I, um," the machete guard looked to her counterpart.

"That should be okay," Spear guard said. "Just don't turn the motorcycle on within the town's limits, yeah? Go ahead," she nodded to the machete guard. "Open the gate."

The machete guard smiled, first to her commander and then to Jedidiah. She turned around, unlatched the gate, and pulled it wide so Jedidiah could push his bike through.

"The little blue house on the end there," the machete guard said, pointing to a quaint home with hand-drawn signs of various cartoon animals and colorful landscapes in the yard. "They've got great soups." And then, with Jedidiah through to the other side, she finished closing the gate again.

"Much appreciated," Jedidiah said through the wooden gate. But he wasn't bound for soup or food of any other kind.

Jedidiah parked his motorcycle next to the fence. It was hexed to run only for those he wished, so Jedidiah had no fear of its being stolen as he searched the village for the reason he'd come. The strength of the magics being used there pulled at him from miles away, long before he'd even approached the gate, but now that he was inside the village, the intensity was causing Jedidiah's eyes to ache. His teeth. His entire head.

The source of his pain was coming from the east side of town, but Jedidiah headed toward the blue house at first, north of the gate, as instructed. He couldn't be sure the guards weren't paying attention. As he walked, though, he cast his eyes toward his right, muttering a minor incantation.

Whatever's going on here, he thought, *it's intense magic.* Twenty steps from the front door of the blue house, home of the great soups, Jedidiah began to veer down the road toward the east. He opened one of the leather pouches at his waist, spared a look toward the gate (nobody seemed to be watching him any longer,) and pulled out a sticky, tacky substance, stretching it between his thumb and forefinger.

"**Phantosos**," Jedidiah whispered, still unsure he wasn't being observed by hidden villagers. At the spoken spell component, the substance began to emanate a purple glow. Jedidiah felt it a safe bet that no others gifted in the magic arts were around, as magic users were few and far between this far north, in his experience. Maybe he was being spied on, but doubtfully by anyone that could see the spellwork pointing him toward why he'd come.

The purple glow began to slowly creep from Jedidiah's finger and work its way in a winding shaft of ectoplasm, guiding him on his path. It crept left and then right, along the edges of falling down houses and past broken, rusted-out pre-Worldfall vehicles. Jedidiah gave cursory glances down the empty streets before following. Daylight–such as existed in a world of skies colored in shades of varying green–cut down on shadows, but there were still plenty of hiding places along his path.

Finally, Jedidiah found himself standing before a ramshackle house at the eastern edge of the village. What had once been the covered front porch of the home had collapsed into rubble, making that entrance completely unusable. A three-foot-high stone wall ran along the southern side of the house, suggesting a pathway that led around back, so Jedidiah snuck that way. As he approached, he could hear someone talking inside the house.

"There was a sleek, black car waiting in front of the library," the voice came, years of practice evident in the narration. "The gods of old only knew what waited behind those tinted windows. Would it be angels of mercy? Or the dark side of divine intervention?"

As Jedidiah came around the house following his mystic compass, he almost ran into a woman standing there. Her slouched shoulders and dirty coveralls suggested to Jedidiah that she'd been maintaining that position for some time. She put her hand up onto Jedidiah's chest and pushed him back forcefully with a hiss. Nestled behind short, black hair, her dark, angry eyes locked onto his.

"Why have you come?" she barked quietly. "You were warned, all but *begged* not to come here!"

Jedidiah let himself be pushed backward, but only for two steps before holding his ground. He smudged the sticky substance between his finger and thumb into a ball and put it back inside a leather pouch at his belt.

"I don't know what you mean," he said.

Don't come to Border Town. DON'T come to Border Town. DON'T COME TO BORDER TOWN! The whispered voice grew harsher, louder, with each wisp of wind that spun around Jedidiah's head.

"Cyn, stop," a man spoke up from behind the woman. He could hardly stand and looked like one solid cough would end him, with too many ribs visible under the skin of his naked upper body.

The voices in the wind disappeared as quickly as they came. Jedidiah shook his head as if to remove any remnants. He snapped his head back up, looking at the woman first, then the man.

"That's right, hotshot," the woman, Cyn, said. "You're *not* the only oneiromancer in town."

The backdoor of the house flew open then, and another older woman in a long country dress of thick material stepped outside onto the stacks of cinder blocks that comprised the back porch. "Cyn, Verrin, back inside! He needs you."

"Stay with this one, Desdra," Cyn said, throwing one last scowl at Jedidiah before heading into the house. "Verrin, let's go."

The frail man gave Jedidiah a soft look and a quick nod before following Cyn inside. The older woman, Desdra, gathered up her dress and stepped off the cinder blocks carefully. She walked over to Jedidiah and gave a simple, almost sad smile.

"Jedidiah Coalstream, I presume?" she offered her hand.

"Seems as though I was expected, if not welcome," Jedidiah said, shaking her hand.

"There *was* some debate on the matter," Desdra said, leading Jedidiah over to some small benches made of stone that sat around a campfire burning inside a ring of rocks. "More harm than good, it was decided, once the mage seemed eager to meet you. Hence Cyn's reaction to your being here. Girl's a stickler when it comes to rules."

"Maybe just start at the beginning," Jedidiah said, trying to make sense of things as they sat down.

"No time for that conversation just now," Desdra said. She flung a handful of powder from her dress's pocket into the flames of the fire. "Better you just have the crash course."

It happened before Jedidiah had locked onto the facts of the situation. The burning powder's fumes were odorless, and no colored smoke accompanied them, but Jedidiah knew then that the fire was inebriated. No, that wasn't it. The fire was his guide in the realm of . . . wherever—the place where sleeping people went. "Let's call it The Beach," he thought. "Sleeping people go to The Beach, and now that's where I am."

Then Desdra was with him. "The Beach," she chuckled. "That's as good a name as any. Careful, now. I threw some extra into the fire to try and keep us out of their hair in the house. Our own little pocket. This way, *no one* is any the wiser to your being here."

Jedidiah liked The Beach, he decided. There were sand and sun, two things that didn't exist in the world as he knew it. Not any longer. Well, the sun *existed*, of course, but you didn't see it in the sky anymore. Also, speaking of the sky, would you look at that! Blue! Jedidiah had forgotten what a blue sky looked like. He hadn't seen one since he was a toddler, after all.

"Jedidiah?" Desdra called him over to sit down with her again. This time it was at a blue picnic table. That's nice.

"Everything here is blue," Jedidiah said, smiling.

"All right, okay," Desdra held a finger up in front of Jedidiah's face. "Look right here, yeah? And, *now*!"

Jedidiah blinked, regaining his focus, his sense, in the dream.

"That," Jedidiah began to stand up. "Was uncalled for. You could have told me you were going to use Blind Dust."

Desdra gently took his arm and guided him back to sit beside her. "I know, but, as I said, we've no time. I had to get the ball rolling. This way, you can fully understand, and maybe a minute will have gone by out there." she pointed past the sunny beach toward the house that Cyn and Verrin had entered.

Jedidiah retook his seat. "Okay, show me."

"Beg your forgiveness," Desdra said, waving her hand at the sand on the beach. "But I lack great skill in oneiromancy."

The sand began to shift and spin as the blue sky turned first gray behind it on the horizon, then black. The sand became a stage, the sun above house lights in a theater. A young woman, a teen, walked into the scene. Darwyn was her name, Darwyn Hess. Darwyn had only recently, mere weeks ago, began to exhibit signs of oneiromancy.

But she wasn't happy about it. Oneiromancy meant

that she wouldn't be trained to fight with weapons.

Wouldn't get to go on patrol in the protection of

Border Town.

Her home.

No, dreamers stayed indoors in hopes of

honing their gift. Inhaling invisible smoke and

eating wild plants. Day after day, praying that, with

practice, they'd tap into the ability of True Sight. Of

precognition.

It was no way to live if you asked Darwyn.

She'd do anything to be rid of it altogether.

Would you really? came the voice one day in a

dream. The mage. His deep, dark skin and short,

white beard. The only hair on his body. *Anything?*

Darwyn said yes. It was a simple enough deal, after all. If she gave the mage her oneiromancy, the mage would see to it that she was the greatest hero Border Town had ever seen. She would be the hero who could *fly*.

So, over the weeks, and without telling anyone else about it, Darwyn practiced with the mage. Little by little giving up her gift–her curse–in favor of a better one. Until one day, the mage said she was ready. She merely had to climb a high enough perch and jump. Their deal would finalize the moment Darwyn flew off into history.

Only the mage had lied.

Darwyn realized almost instantly as she fell that the mage had tricked her. In her fear, she used what little oneiromancy she had left to shield herself from the death that waited below. It was the fear that caught Fred's attention. Fred, the most practiced oneiromancer in all of the Border Town region, came down from his ridge to find Darwyn's wrecked body. Still alive, but barely.

Once they got Darwyn home, Fred began his work. Darwyn was trapped inside her body by the mage, who himself was trying to be reborn inside the girl. Fred told Darwyn stories day and night. Any and all kinds of stories to nourish the girl's spirit while other oneiromancers, Cyn and Verrin, tried their best to aid Fred when his spirit's energy waned. But the end was coming soon, one way or another.

Then the stage, the players, everything that made up the scenes that had been playing in front of Jedidiah disappeared. His surroundings began to look like the unkempt backyard that he had initially sat down in.

"It's wearing off," Desdra explained. "Hopefully, you've heard enough."

"You didn't get to the part about why I got warned off from coming," Jedidiah said.

"**Allow me to explain, then,**" a man said from behind them. Desdra flew from the bench, across the yard, and into a small shed with a crunching sound. Jedidiah turned just enough to see who was there before he was held fast in place. It was the man from the dream play Desdra had shown.

The mage.

"**How did it happen? Many paths led to this place. It *not* happening would have made for a more impressive tale, honestly. You play the cards that you're dealt, it seems, even before you**

understand the game." The mage walked around the yard as he talked, as though he were stretching his legs.

"**I've spent two weeks in a prison that, from the outside, seemed perfectly escapable. My cell consisted of naught, but muscle, blood, and bone, and my warden was a squishy organ composed entirely of gray matter.**" He looked at his hand, wiggling his fingers as if for the first time. "**I, Ja'drune, kept in such a manner! Unthinkable. It's this dream magic, you understand—this oneiromancy. I'm unaccustomed to such a lack of boundaries. Blood magic, *my* area of expertise, comes from a more base, *solid* place. Less . . . frivolous.**"

Jedidiah listened as the mage spoke. Unable to move, he didn't really have any choice to do otherwise. But, as this Ja'drune gave his speech, Jedidiah could follow him around the yard with his eyes. *Okay, then.* Jedidiah thought, hard, ignoring his role as an audience member and looking to his belt. *The Dust is starting to wear off. If I can just get to my pouches, I think I can–*

"**You could what?**" Ja'drune asked, appearing before Jedidiah, a furious scowl across his face. "**We're in the Dreaming. No unguarded thought goes unheard here, fool. And I thought you were better than this–a sorcerer of this age. Yet here you are, merely a charlatan with a hodgepodge bag of contrivances–a dabbler. Such a letdown.**"

Ja'drune, with a wave of his arm, levitated Jedidiah up from the bench and floated him in the air, walking around his quarry as he talked. "**Oh, yes, I've been watching from afar. The** motorcycle mystic. Wielder of the Sable. I imagine now that you merely stole that harmonica. One who stands with the Cabal of Song would not find himself so easily dispatched.**" The blood mage let out a sigh. "**But *I'll* have your paltry tricks now, Jedidiah Coalstream. Die knowing that you do not measure up to the legend surrounding you.**" And Ja'drune grabbed Jedidiah's belt, attempting to rip it free.

Then an explosion of red and orange light took over everything. Jedidiah briefly felt his body begin to fall to the ground, but he was already lying beside the stone bench at his next conscious thought. He looked around to find Ja'drune, who was missing the right side of his face, being pulled back toward the house in tendrils of green and yellow energies. An astral image of a young teen girl stood behind him, reeling him in. The mage's right eye dangled from its socket, and he coughed evil, pained whispers from the gore of his mangled, scorched mouth.

"**Trickster!**" he barked, then laughed maniacally, pointing at Jedidiah with the stub of his handless right arm. "**We've not finished! I'll escape this . . . bag of . . . meat. Soon! And I will find . . . you . . . oh, how I will find you!**"

And with his ominous threat given, Ja'drune, the blood mage, disappeared back inside the house of one Darwyn Hess, hero of Border Town.

*　*　*　*　*

Darwyn was propped up in her bed on a sea of loaned pillows. For two days, she'd slept dreamlessly, all the more thankful for it. That morning, a small dream had come. It wasn't visual but emotional. Just the feeling of rage briefly lit before she startled awake. Jedidiah, who was seated in a chair that was too small for his frame, looked at her as she woke.

"Fred, Cyn, she's awake," he called over his shoulder. Candles burned, had *been* burning for some time from the looks of them, around the room. Jedidiah rose from his chair to inspect Darwyn's right arm. "May I?"

Darwyn looked down to her arm to discover it wrapped in a cast of hard mud. She nodded to Jedidiah, who examined her hand, testing if she felt his touch on her fingertips. When she said that she could, he let out a breath he'd been holding.

"Get away from her already!" Cyn bellowed from the doorway, entered, and took Jedidiah's place at the young girl's side. "Give her some air, Coalstream."

"She's better, Cincinnati," a slight, wrinkled man, balding with wisps of gray hair at the side of his head, came behind Cyn. "She's awake, now. So she's getting better. No need to go shouting in the house."

"Sorry, Fred," Cyn mumbled.

"Cincinnati?" Jedidiah said through a big smile that he half-heartedly tried hiding.

"It's Cyn to you, Coalstream!" Cyn yelled, turning to face Jedidiah. Fred pushed through the two of them and made his way to hold Darwyn's hand.

"You *are* feeling better now, ain'tcha?" Fred asked with an eye raised in question.

"I, I think so," Darwyn answered. "I'm not entirely sure what happened, though. But," she took a beat to think it over, but continued shakily, "there was a man. He . . . he had a white beard. And his eyes–" but she lost where that sentence ended, so fell silent.

"Ja'drune," Jedidiah said. "His name is Ja'drune."

Fred hissed, then spit on the floor. He muttered some words that Jedidiah couldn't catch. "We don't give that monster any more power here than he already has," Fred said. He motioned to Cyn, who came to take his place at the bed. "Can we have a word outside?" he asked Jedidiah.

Jedidiah followed the old man out the back door, down from the cinder blocks, and toward the stone benches around the fire pit. Fred sat, but this time Jedidiah stood.

"That poor little one," Fred started, poking into the ashes of the spent fire with a slender pole. "Has a tough road in front of her. Not least of which is going to be finding out that two people she knew since she was knee-high died in the service of saving her from that monster." Fred spat again. "Two friends. Now, we'll do the tending there. Shendra and Verrin weren't kin, but they might as well aught've been. You," Fred looked at Jedidiah but couldn't meet his eyes. "I think it's time you moved on from here. See if maybe the bastard follows."

Jedidiah quietly agreed and made to leave. But Darwyn was standing at the back door, tears streaming down her face. She pushed off Cyn, who was trying to hold her up and leaned into the door frame.

"Shendra, Fred?" she sobbed. "And Verrin?"

"It's not your fault," Fred said. He got up and walked past Jedidiah, heading to Darwyn.

"Enough!" Darwyn shouted. "Enough. I can still feel him, even though he's far away now. He's *so* angry. But then," through her gritted teeth, "so am I." She stepped away from the door frame and staggered. Cyn caught her quick. "You, Mr. Coalstream. Fred kept me safe, wrapped up in his stories, while the others held him, *Ja'drune,* at bay," she snarled his name. "Spent their lives on me for the stupid thing I done. But you, you *hurt* him. How did you do that?"

Fred and Cyn joined Darwyn in looking at Jedidiah.

"I'm not like you," Jedidiah began. "I mean, I'm not an oneiromancer."

"You cast that Second Sight spell," Cyn said. "We all saw you do it."

"But your belt, when you tricked him into grabbing it," Fred chimed in. "*That* wasn't a spell of our kind. That was–"

"Elemental magic," Jedidiah interrupted. He reached to his belt and turned it over, showing a thin black root woven into the belt's intricate design. "It's hexed. And bound with Blood magic."

"Teach me," Darwyn said.

"Darwyn!" Fred and Cyn yelled at the same time.

The teen somehow found the strength to hold up her hand, shushing the pair. She was fading again, fast. Darwyn slid down Cyn to her knees, all the while never losing eye contact with Jedidiah.

While she hadn't the energy to stand, her voice did

not waver when she repeated, "Teach me."

"I'm sorry," Jedidiah said, walking over to the

girl. "Elemental magic, maybe someone could teach

you, I don't know. But I'm not your guy. And Blood

magic, that's not something that can be taught. It's

not like what you can do, where–"

"Then Fred's right," Darwyn said, tears falling

down her cheeks again. "Just . . . go away."

Jedidiah nodded, first to Darwyn, then to Fred

and Cyn. He began his walk back to his Fat Boy at

the front gate.

"Coalstream, hold up," Cyn shouted from

behind him after he'd gone a couple of blocks.

Jedidiah looked back, waiting for her to catch up to

him. She wore the same stern face, but her eyes

were wet. "I just wanted to–what I mean is, I don't know how things would have played out here. If you hadn't come, I mean."

Jedidiah looked at her. In his silence, she wiped her eyes dry.

"What, um, what I'm saying is, do you think she'll be okay now?" Cyn's stern look slid into a worried one. "She says she can still feel him, right?"

"Could be Fred's plan will work," Jedidiah said. He began to walk again. "Maybe Ja'drune will follow me away from here. Live bait. But, and I'm sorry," he stopped to look Cyn in the eye. "He's still got a toehold in her mind. Will he use it again? I don't know. She understands what he's about now, so it would be a fight." Jedidiah began to walk away again. "I've got a friend, south of here. Far south. If anyone knows what should happen next, it'll be her.

Meet me in The Kingdom one month from now, at

Tuggett's Knee, and I'll tell you what I find out."

Cyn grabbed Jedidiah's shoulder and came

around in front of him, "One month, Coalstream,

I'm holding you to that. I'll be there."

Jedidiah looked at her, then looked at her hand

on his shoulder until she released it. "It's not a

promise that I'll know anything more, Cyn. Just that

I'll ask."

"I understand," Cyn said.

Jedidiah got to his motorcycle then and

pushed it through the gate once the guards had fully

opened the way.

"Take care of yourself, Cyn," he said, putting

his helmet on.

"You as well, Coalstream," Cyn said. "Safe journeys and gentle storms."

Jedidiah nodded assent at the customary farewell, started his motorcycle, and headed out. He'd gotten almost two kilometers from where he'd left Cyn when his radio chirped. He sighed and answered.

"Yes?"

"It's Fred," Jedidiah thought that the old man sounded tired. Then he admitted to himself that he was, too.

"I'm gone," Jedidiah said.

"I know. I just wanted to thank you properly for your help. Felt like we parted poorly, and that wasn't what I was aiming for." Fred paused. "Maybe someday, really soon, you can come back when things are–"

"We're good, Fred," Jedidiah interrupted. "Anything else?"

"Well, just . . ." Fred was quiet for so long that Jedidiah thought he'd lost the signal. When his voice came back over the radio, it was cloaked in concern. "The Cabal of Song. Dream magic. Elemental magic, and even Blood. How much trouble you in, son?"

In response, Jedidiah switched the radio off, revved his motorcycle, and rode away from Border Town into the night.

*   *   *   *   *

Explore more of the world of Harrowed Earth in Book Two of the ongoing series, *Cicero Wants You*!

The Kingdom, grown from what was once Kansas City, Missouri, is as far west as one can travel in what had been the United States before feeling the effects of The Shift. It's a metropolis by way of cavalcade. With a working water refinery, gasoline production, and proximity to The Shift that seems to keep it beneath Ravok-Dyn notice, The Kingdom draws people from all over North America to its expanding walls. Made up of individual baronies with ever-changing allegiances to each other, The Kingdom comprises the last known vestiges of the human race.

Tuggett's Knee and Renaissance, two neighboring baronies within The Kingdom, Seemingly at philosophical odds–the former with an eye to the future, the latter steeped in the past–yet growing together. Citizens of each barony will need to rise, standing united against what's coming for them and the whole of The Kingdom.

It's a new day in a fallen world.

And an excerpt from the continuing adventures of Jedidiah Coalstream in Harrowed Earth Book Three: *Sordid Deals.*

The Children Have Come

Muddy Rum region

East of Lexington, Kentucky, PW (Pre-Worldfall)

"Beyond this house, the Earth is not as you picture it to be from your Ma's stories," the Elder Ma explained, silver hair escaping from her hurried bun in straggled wisps. She sat before a fire that burned low, whispering to three of her kin; two young boys and their Ma, who was not the Elder Ma's own child but a seed-holder, which made her family. One boy had the colorings of his Ma, pale white skin and thick black hair. Dark brown eyes. The other boy, though, had skull short blond hair, and his skin was teal-colored. This boy went shirtless, while his brother dressed in a worn cotton top that had a faded metal bird on it and read *TOUR OF THE WORLD VAN HALEN 1984*. All three stood around a small, shabby wooden kitchen table, listening as the older woman quietly spoke.

"You boys, we've been blessed, living here as we have. Your Elder Pa, rest his soul, had the foresight to keep us going. He knew the Science for Freshwater—for taking what comes from above and making it safe for drinking and using in the gardens."

"Then why are we leaving if it's so safe for us here?" the shirted boy asked loudly.

"Hush, now," his Ma whispered back, taking the boy by either shoulder and pulling him close, her face to his. "Your Elder Ma told you quiet's what's called for, didn't she?" She dropped her hands to her dirty blue jeans and absently worked a frayed belt loop, waiting for the older woman to continue.

After a moment of staring down her grandson with a withering look, the Elder Ma began again.

"Your Pa has seen signs of Children in the forest surrounding the back pasture," she said, hardly speaking the words aloud. The boy's Pa, Marcus, the Elder Ma's son, had explained everything the night before. He didn't have the education that she and her late husband had, but they did their best under apocalyptic circumstances, so her boy was nobody's fool. She waved her shirtless grandson over to her. "He thinks they've

come for Dekken."

www.ingramcontent.com/pod-product-compliance
Lightning Source LLC
Chambersburg PA
CBHW052141220626
47052CB00005B/1147